WHEEL AWAY!

by **Dayle Ann Dodds**

illustrations by **Thacher Hurd**

HarperTrophy

A Division of HarperCollinsPublishers

Library of Congress Cataloging-in-Publication Data

Dodds, Dayle Ann.

   Wheel away!

   Summary: A runaway wheel takes a bouncy, bumpy, amusing journey through town.

   [1. Wheels—Fiction.   2. Stories in rhyme]

I. Hurd, Thacher, ill.   II. Title.

PZ8.3.D645Wh   1989   [E]   87-27091

ISBN 0-06-021688-3

ISBN 0-06-21689-1 (lib. bdg.)

ISBN 0-06-443267-X (pbk.)

First Harper Trophy edition, 1991.

Oh no! See it go!

pa-da-rump

pa-da-rump

pa-da-rump-pump-pump

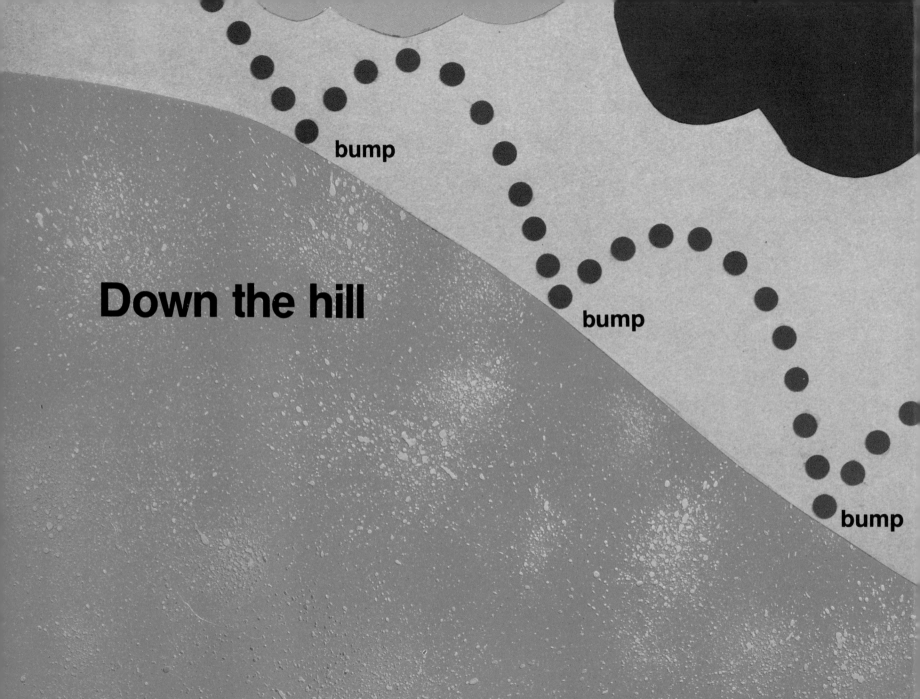

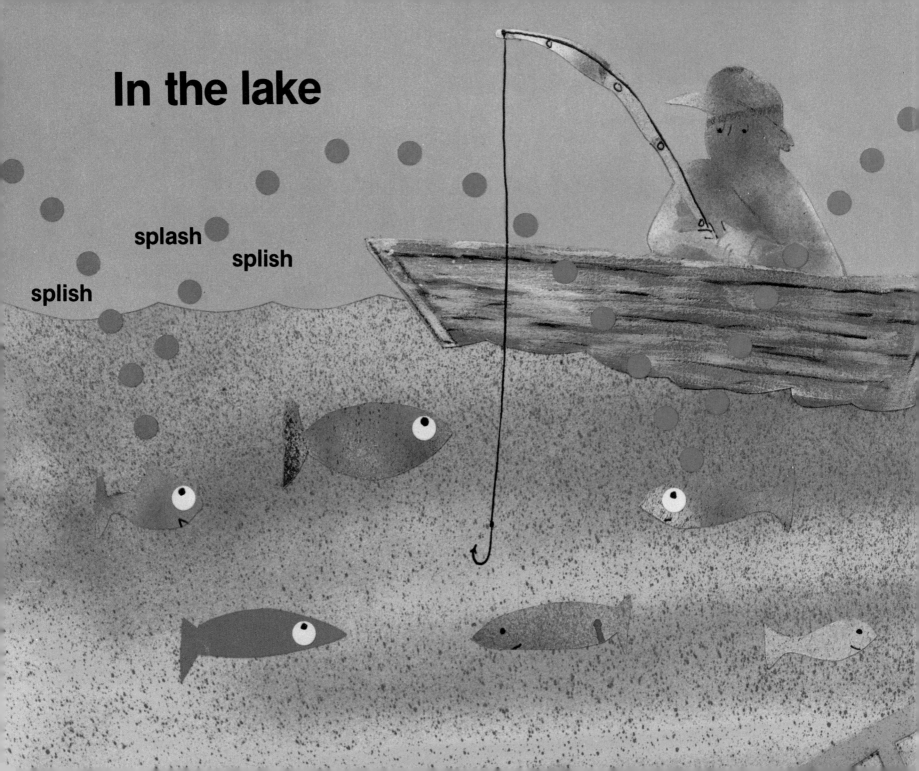

In the lake

splash

splish

splish

zip

zap

zip

Under the shirts

whip

whap

whip

Across the dirt

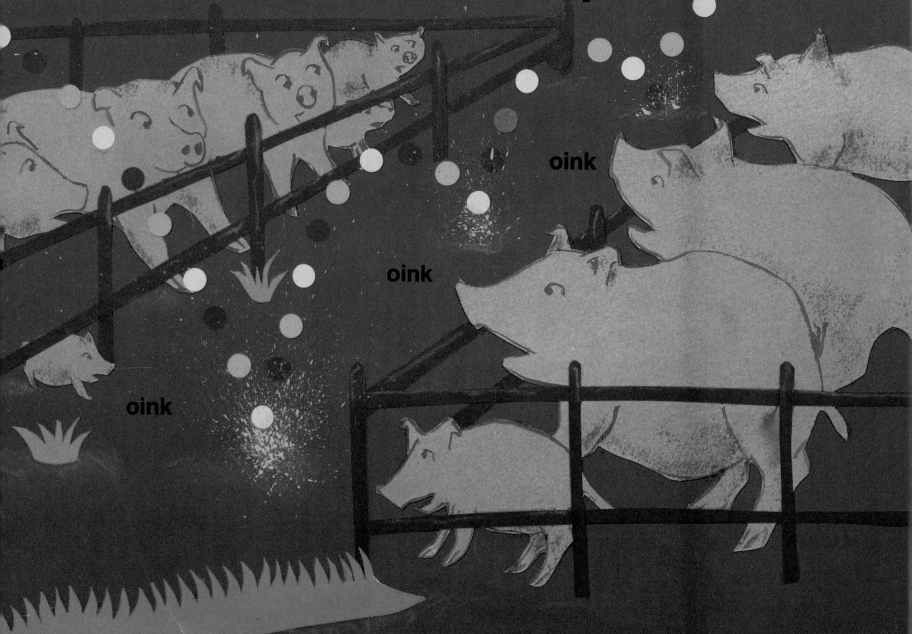

On top of the hens

boink

boink

boink

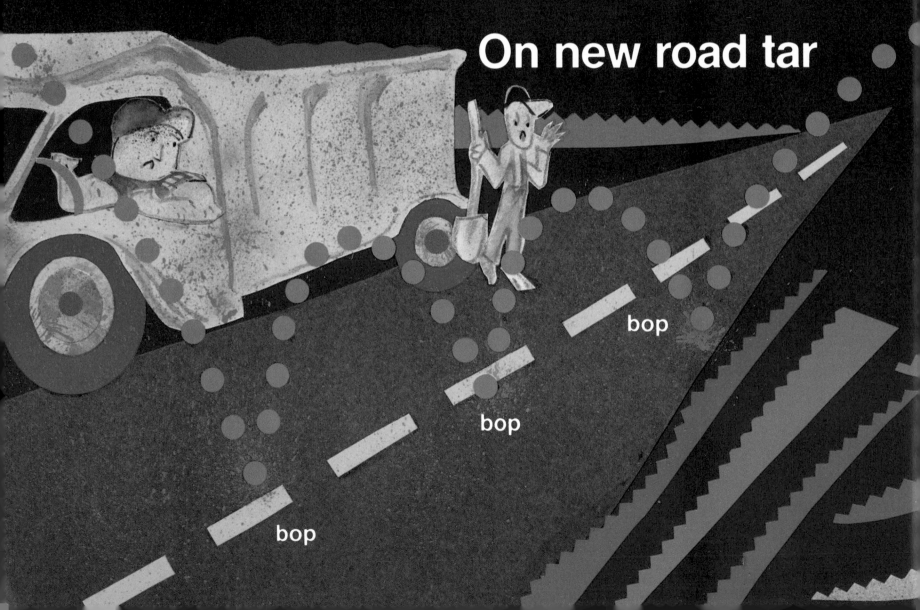

Over paint cans

squirt

squirt

squirt

Under paint man

splirt

splirt

In front of the truck

clickety-clack

In back of the duck

quackety-quack

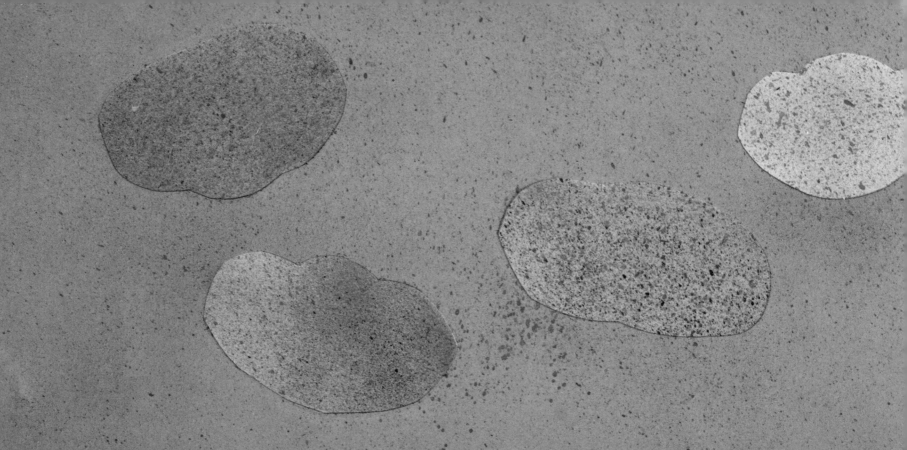

slowing

slowing slowing slowing

Oh no!

Coming back!

pa-da-rump pa-da-rump

pa-da-rump-pump-pump

quackety-quack

clickety-clack

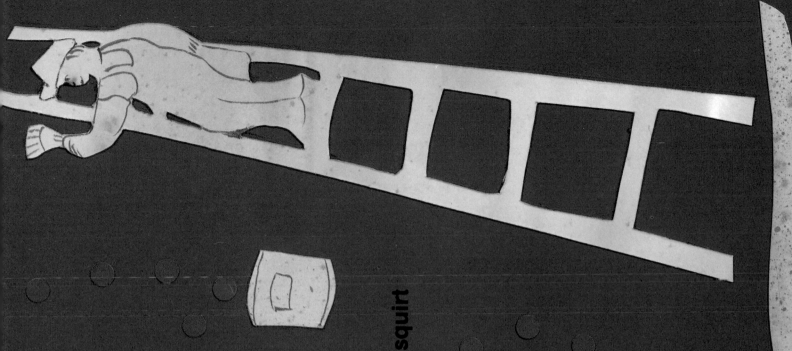

squirt

squirt

squirt

splirt

splirt

splirt

splirt

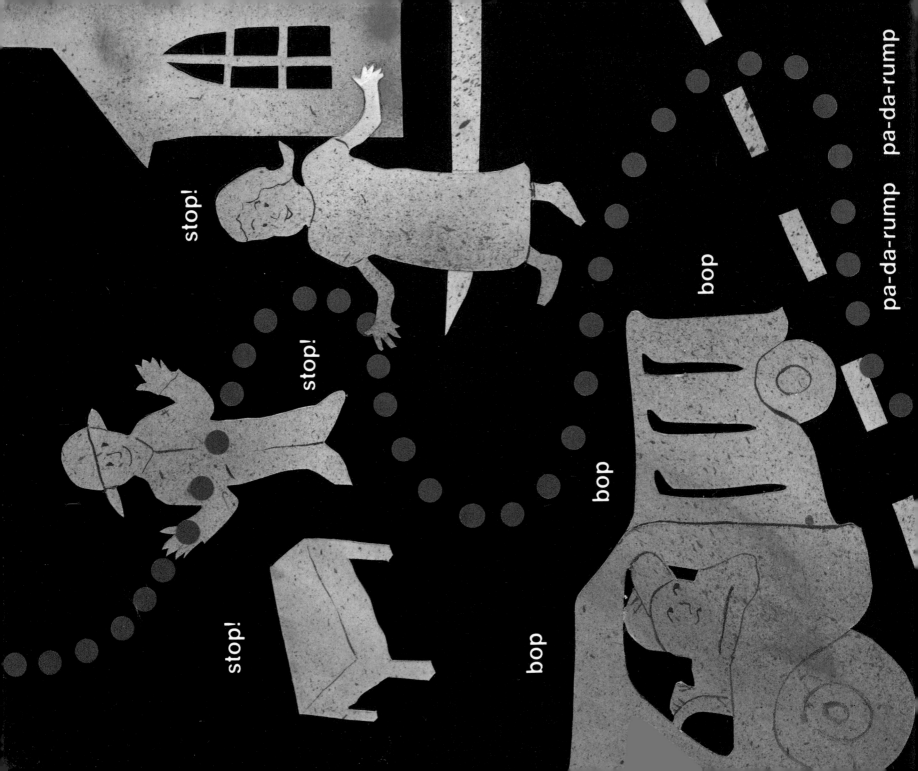

pa-da-rump-pump-pump

boink

boink

boink

oink

oink

oink

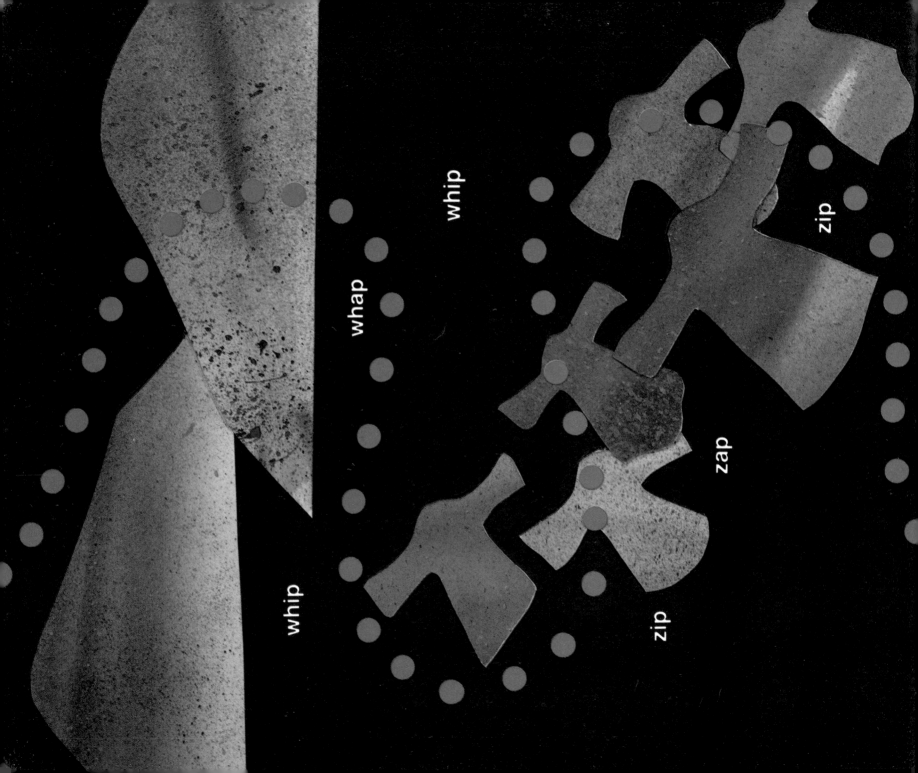

whip

whap

whip

zip

zap

whip

zip

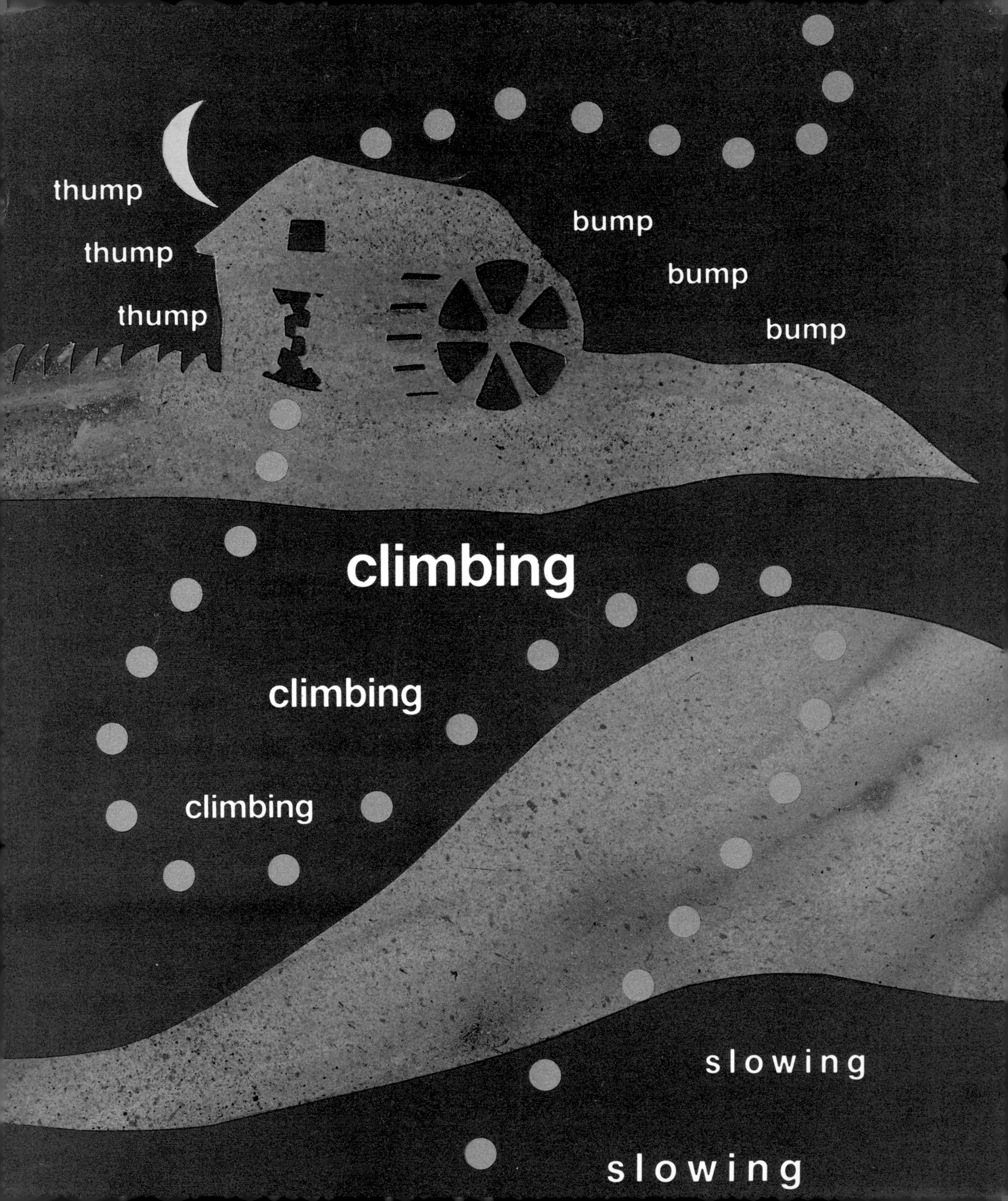
thump
thump
thump
bump
bump
bump
climbing
climbing
climbing
slowing
slowing

slowing

back.